SOLO SOUNDS

FOR TRUMPET

Solos with Piano Accompaniment-Levels 3-5   **Volume 1**

Cover Credit: Ace Music Center, North Miami, Florida
Yamaha International Corporation Musical Instrument Division

Editor: Jack Lamb

EL03342

Elegy

Major Herman Vincent

Twin Stars

Carl Frangkiser

6

Ayre

Jeremiah Clarke
Arranged by Howard Cable
Edited by Bobby Herriot

Chorale Melody No. 19

J.S. Bach
Arranged by Leonard B. Smith

Contempora Suite
(For Leonard B. Smith)

Gordon Young (ASCAP)

PRELUDE

Moderato

ALLEMANDE

Allegro marcato

14

SARABANDE

GIGUE

Polka

Major Herman Vincent

D. S. al Coda

D. S. al Coda

⊕ Coda

poco rit.

⊕ Coda

poco rit.

(For Robert V. Peterson)

Chamade
(March Heroique)

Leonard B. Smith (ASCAP)

*A signal made by a parley, by beat of drum or sound of trumpet.

Special Delivery

Bobby Herriot and
Howard Cable

Bright - with spirit (about ♩ = 112)

28

(To Ross Mulholland)
Fiesta Time

Leonard B. Smith

(To William A. Fox)

Bourrée In The Style Of Handel

Leonard B. Smith (ASCAP)

Carnival Of Venice

Arranged by Fred Weber

Var. I

Variation 2

La Casa

Gerald Knipfel and
Beldon Leonard

Allegretto

Tempo di Valse

40

El Verano

Gerald Knipfel and
Beldon Leonard

Andante con moto

Andante espressivo

E Allegro con brio